#50513
BL4
As1

Fox Eyes

by Mordicai Gerstein

For Susan and Risa with fox-eyed love
M.G.

Library of Congress Cataloging-in-Publication Data
Gerstein, Mordicai.
Fox eyes / written and illustrated by Mordicai Gerstein.
    p.   cm. — (Road to reading. Mile 5)
Summary: Martin's great aunt warns him about looking too long into the eyes
of a fox, but he can't resist and finds himself in the fox's body for a day.
ISBN 0-307-26509-9 (pbk.) — ISBN 0-307-46509-8 (GB)
[1. Foxes—Fiction. 2. Human-animal communication—Fiction. 3.
Identity—Fiction. 4. Magic—Fiction. 5. Grandmothers—Fiction.] I. Title.
II. Series.
PZ7.G325 Fr 2000
[Fic]—dc21   00-034776

A GOLDEN BOOK · New York
Golden Books Publishing Company, Inc. New York, New York 10106

ISBN: 0-307-26509-9 (pbk)
ISBN: 0-307-46509-8 (GB)

10 9 8 7 6 5 4 3 2 1

Contents

1. The Wooden Fish   1

2. Aunt Zavella   6

3. August   11

4. A Little Trick   16

5. Chicken and Dumplings   29

6. The Fox and the Fiddle   42

7. The Vixen   50

8. The Music Lesson   57

9. The Old Country   65

10. Magic   69

1

The Wooden Fish

The fox followed his nose through the afternoon woods. It was an especially long, pointed nose, and it told him he was getting close. He smelled chickens, woodsmoke, melting apples, blueberries, and butter. His mouth began to water.

He stopped at the edge of the woods where the grass began. There was the house, huge and ugly like all human things. In front of it was the chicken coop with its little chicken-wire yard. Oh, those plump cluckers!

The fox had his heart set on a white hen that always pecked near the fence. It looked particularly stupid and tasty. And there, sitting atop the chicken coop as if she owned it, was that fat, vain cat. He had watched her spend hours licking her black fur. His own coat glowed like the sun with hardly any care at all.

The fox decided to try flattery. "Good afternoon, you gorgeous creature," he said in the cat language. Like all foxes, he spoke most animal languages. He had just a hint of fox accent.

"Oh, it's you again," hissed the cat. She puffed up her fur and dug her claws into the chicken coop roof. "Forget your flattery! You will *never* taste my chickens!"

Foxes are not usually afraid of cats. But this cat was almost as large as he was. He *would* taste those chickens, but he needed a plan.

His thoughts were interrupted by human voices. He smelled a new scent and looked up at the house.

Yes!

There in the window at the top of the house he saw the face of a young human. A boy. The fox's mother had told him about young humans and the thing that could happen if you looked into their eyes.

"Have you ever wanted to be human?" the fox asked the cat.

"Why would I?" sneered the cat. "They are my slaves. They feed me the finest food, house me in this palace, and all I have to do is keep you away from *my* chickens."

The boy saw the fox and pointed straight at him. Behind the boy stood the old woman who lived in the house. She spoke and the boy listened. Human was the one language the fox couldn't understand.

She was smart, that old woman. He had watched her often over the years. The fox could tell by the way she looked at him that she knew things. And sometimes, for no reason, she made odd sounds. Beautiful, high, wailing sounds, like birds or the wind.

Now the boy was holding something. Was it a gun? The fox tensed to run. His mother had told him about guns.

The thing the boy was holding looked like a wooden fish. He also held some kind of stick. The boy scraped the stick on the wooden fish and the fox's fur stood on end. His ears and tail tingled.

The boy was making noises with the wooden things. Noises something like the old woman's wailing. Strange, amazing noises. The fox sat down.

He listened.

2

Aunt Zavella

The very first day Martin came to stay with Great Aunt Zavella in her grand, rickety, old house in the mountains, he looked out the window of his room and saw the fox.

"Look, Auntie! A real fox!" The only wild animals he'd seen before were in zoos.

"Yes," said his great aunt, "I know that one. I call him Sharpnose. He wants to taste my chickens." She laughed. "But he never will because Zanzibar guards them. Zanzibar is my cat. She's fierce."

Aunt Zavella's face was brown and

wrinkled. Her eyes were as black and shiny as two baked raisins. She wore long skirts and flowered blouses and kerchiefs.

"It's how we dressed in the Old Country," she always said. "That's where I come from." She looked to Martin like a life-size frosted gingerbread cookie.

"But Martin," said Aunt Zavella, "there is one thing you must always remember. . . ." She leaned her face, brown and wrinkled as an old paper bag, close to his. He was surprised at how suddenly serious she became.

"You must never," she said, "*ever* look too long into the eyes of a fox."

"Why not?" he asked.

She chuckled and nodded her head.

"Certain foxes will play a little trick on you."

"What little trick, Auntie?"

"This little trick . . . that little trick. . . ." She touched her finger to his nose. "Just be careful."

Martin had no idea what she was talking about. But he felt a chill run down his spine.

Martin's parents had driven him the long distance up from the city where they lived. He was going to spend all of August with his great aunt, while his parents stayed in the city and worked.

Aunt Zavella's house sat in a meadow surrounded by woods and mountains. The house smelled of cinnamon honey cake and was so full of rooms it was hard to count them all.

There were big rooms, little rooms, dark ones, and bright ones. But the best room was at the very top of the house and it was Martin's. It was small and painted yellow. It had wonderful slanted ceilings and a window seat on which to sit and watch a fox.

3

August

Martin's parents had said the only thing he must do that August was practice the violin every day for half an hour after lunch. He had been taking lessons ever since he was little. The violin was one Aunt Zavella had brought from the Old Country years ago. She had given it to Martin.

Martin played well, but lately he was bored with playing. He would have forgotten all about the violin if he didn't *have* to practice. It helped that every day, while Martin practiced, he saw Sharpnose from the window. Sometimes he was sure the fox was listening to his music.

The fox stood where the woods shadowed the lawn. It would look up at Martin, then glance at Zanzibar sitting atop the chicken coop, and then back at Martin again. When it looked at Martin, Martin looked back into its yellow-gold eyes. But Martin was always careful not to look too long.

Making music for a fox was more fun than just practicing. Martin sometimes played for almost an hour. Then he put away the violin and was completely free. Free to explore the mossy, root-tangled paths through the woods and mountains with Aunt Zavella.

Aunt Zavella seemed to be friends with each rock and bird, each plant and squirrel. Martin wondered if she was some kind

of wizard. She showed Martin how to walk without a sound by not stepping on twigs or dried leaves. She taught him to see things out of the corners of his eyes while looking straight ahead. She told him the names of all the trees, flowers, birds, and animals, in English and in her magical-sounding Old Country language. Martin remembered almost all of them.

"In the woods," said Aunt Zavella, "animals look like plants or rocks, and plants and rocks look like animals. Sometimes one thing turns into another when you get close to it."

Martin knew exactly what she meant. A certain big, brown bear always turned into a boulder when Martin got close enough to touch its furry moss. And often, a bush that looked just like a porcupine turned out actually to be one.

Martin also hiked alone to the tops of mountains. He met wild animals, showered under waterfalls, and swam in secret stream-fed pools. Martin loved this whole, fat, green month of August. He wished it would go on forever. And for a while, it seemed as if it would.

4

A Little Trick

But August always ends. Suddenly it was the last afternoon of the last day of the month. The next morning, Martin's parents would come for him. Together they'd drive back to the city where the only animals were dogs on leashes and cats on couches.

Martin missed his parents and longed to see them, but he also knew how much he would miss Aunt Zavella, her house, and the wonderful, wild world that surrounded it. Before leaving, he had to say good-bye to the woods and all its creatures.

He took his favorite trail, zipping his jacket against an autumn chill that hadn't been there yesterday. Aunt Zavella said summer was just a temporary guest in these mountains. But winter was always there, hiding behind the highest ridge, waiting to slip back and take over again.

A rabbit hopped into Martin's path and stopped. Martin didn't breathe until it hopped again and vanished.

"Good-bye, rabbit," he whispered.

A little farther on, a bush turned into a woodchuck and slowly waddled away.

"Good-bye, woodchuck."

Martin tried to sneak up to his bear before it turned into a boulder, but he wasn't quite quick enough.

"Good-bye, bear." He patted the moss where the bear's nose should have been.

Martin followed the path around a huge old maple growing out of a split rock. That's when he saw the fox.

It trotted briskly along the path. It seemed not to know that Martin was right behind. Its coat flashed like fire in the patches of sun that spattered the afternoon shade.

I'm *sure* this is Sharpnose, thought Martin. He had to swallow a giggle as he silently tiptoed along in step behind the fox.

There was joy and excitement, being this close to something so wild. Then, wishing his heart wasn't pounding so loudly, Martin took bigger steps, to see just how close he could get.

He got closer and saw the fox's ear twitch at a gnat. He got closer still and could see every gleaming hair in the fox's gold-orange coat. And when Martin was close enough to touch the fox's tail with a broomstick (if he'd had one), a stream crossed the path and the fox stopped. Martin, taken by surprise, almost tripped over the fox's tail.

The fox turned and saw Martin behind it. It didn't run. The fox stood in the path and looked directly into Martin's eyes.

Martin remembered Aunt Zavella's warning about looking into the eyes of a fox. It's probably, he thought, just some Old Country superstition. What could possibly happen?

To be honest—which Martin was—he doubted many of his great aunt's stories. Up until now, he'd always been careful, when looking at the fox, not to look into its eyes for too long. But this was his last day, and how would he ever know the truth unless he tried? So, at the moment when he knew he should look away, he didn't.

Martin and the fox stood there for what seemed a long time. Not moving, just looking deep, deep into each other's eyes. There was a flicker in the fox's eyes, like yellow fire. After a while, Martin thought he saw secret caves, a world of hidden places under the twisted roots of ancient trees where small creatures trembled and waited.

Martin blinked and now the fox's eyes were brown. Slowly Martin realized he was no longer looking at the fox. He was staring at another boy. It was as if the fox had slipped away somehow, and this boy

had taken its place. The boy's jacket, shirt, and pants were just like Martin's. There was even something familiar about the boy's face.

It was Martin's face! Martin was looking at himself.

Martin glanced down and was startled, first at how close the ground was, and then at the two little black paws where his hands should have been. The fox *had* played a trick on him! What was it?

"Ha!" cried the other boy. "Ha! I got you!" He sounded exactly like Martin.

"Every day," said the boy, "I've watched you and listened to you. And every day, I've plotted and wondered—how can I get him to look into my eyes a little too long? Even just a second too long?"

Completely confused, Martin tried to

make sense of what this "other Martin" was saying. Who was this boy?

"And then I thought," the boy continued, "I know! I'll let him follow me—and you did! I'll let him get close—and you did! Now, I thought—if I can just hold his eyes... and I got you! Yahoooo!"

The boy jumped into the air, did a back flip, landed in a handstand, and danced on his hands in circles. Martin couldn't do any of those things.

Then Martin understood the fox's trick—he'd traded places. The fox was in Martin's body and Martin was in the fox's. Martin looked behind him and saw the long, orange, white-tipped tail that was now his. He wagged it and felt an odd thrill.

"Look!" cried the fox boy, startling

Martin. "I have fingers! Now I can do what you do! YaHOOO!" He grabbed up handfuls of leaves and threw them into the air like confetti. "And look at YOU! What a gorgeous fox you are! Oh, you'll love being a fox. You'll have tons of fun!" shouted the fox boy. "I know you will!"

A chipmunk streaked past and, without thinking, Martin was after it. He ran and felt as if he was flying. He'd never moved so fast. He was sure he could run like this forever. He heard the fox boy's laughter behind him, fading and weaving into the sounds of birds, crickets, and fluttering leaves.

"I'm a fox!" barked Martin joyously. "I'm *really* a fox!"

But he was still himself, too—seeing, hearing, and smelling with the eyes, ears, and nose of a fox! The air was thick with rustles, squeaks, squawks, and whistles, and the scents of rotting leaves, earth, water, mice, and even worms. It was like being in the middle of an ocean of sounds and smells. And the fox's senses told him what they all were.

He heard layers of sounds that were muttered questions and chattered answers, whistled invitations and buzzed warnings. He heard jays bursting berries. He heard grasshoppers chewing grass. He heard the fluttering pulses of dozens of tiny beating hearts.

And everything he heard, he could also smell. The smells were so vivid, he could almost see them, as if each had a color and shape. And wherever a sound and scent came together, he knew *that's* where a chipmunk is. *There's* a sparrow. *There's* a baby rabbit. *There's* a hive of bees. And as he ran, he began to see the things he heard and smelled.

He smelled, heard, and then saw a snake, a black one, and he was after it. It stayed just ahead of his pointing nose, going as fast as it could, zig-zagging, slipping under leaves and branches. It suddenly disappeared down a hole under the roots of a tree.

Martin snuffled and pawed at the hole. He wanted that snake.

"You can come out now," he whispered to it. "I just want to talk to you. You don't have to be afraid. I'm a snake, just like you."

Martin was surprised at himself. He was lying. Martin almost never lied, and

here he was speaking a soft, hissing snake language and lying to a snake. It was fun being foxy! He listened at the hole and heard the snake's tongue flicking out again and again.

"That fox is gone," Martin hissed to the snake. "I'm your friend. Oh, please come and play. . . ."

But just then, a little way off, Martin caught sight of another chipmunk. It was sitting up on a fallen log, crunching noisily on an acorn.

Martin lowered his body closer to the ground, aimed his nose and caught the sweet, plump smell of the little body. Silently, he began to creep toward it. He wanted that chipmunk. He had no idea why, but he wanted that chipmunk.

5

Chicken and Dumplings

Meanwhile, Sharpnose in Martin's body skipped, twirled, and tap-danced through the woods and back toward the house. He clapped his hands and did cartwheels and handsprings. He leaped up and swung from the branches of trees.

All the while, he was still a fox, with a fox's mind. And his fox mind was amazed at the whirl of thoughts in Martin's head. It was like a den full of butterflies.

Martin's thoughts and memories flew around and around in his head, like little moving pictures. Many made no sense at all to the fox.

What is "The City?" he wondered. There were swarms of words, and each time the fox looked at something in the woods, a word for that thing popped out of his mouth.

Some words were gathered into stories. Some were jokes. The fox laughed when he thought of them, though he wasn't sure why. There was a little box of words called "Old Country" that smelled like cinnamon honey cake.

As he skipped along, he found himself making the same kind of wailing bird noises the old woman sometimes did. It was called singing! The sounds were also a little like the ones Martin's fiddle made. It was called music! It made Sharpnose so happy he twirled faster and skipped higher. He was singing songs!

One was about something called a starspangledbanner. Another, which he liked even better, was about a fox that goes out on a chilly night and catches a goose. Sharpnose heard Martin's stomach growl. It reminded him he hadn't eaten all day.

Sharpnose soon came in sight of the house. He smelled the woodsmoke and roasting chickens, but without his fox nose, the countless other smells were gone. Without fox ears, the clatter of pots and pans sounded soft and less clattery.

It was annoying, but on the other hand—on *both* hands, as a matter of fact—he had all these wiggling fingers! At last, after all these weeks, what he'd longed to do was possible!

He ran leaping and dancing toward the

house and saw Zanzibar running to meet him. But she stopped suddenly. Her back arched high and her black fur bristled.

"Martin," she hissed, "you're not yourself today!"

"But I am," said the fox. "I am most *especially* myself. And you, my dear, are *especially* lovely this evening."

"Yes, it's this evening light," said Zanzibar, giving her tail a lick. "It makes my fur glow. But why are you speaking my language now, when you never have before?"

"I just learned it, and I wanted to surprise you," said the fox.

"I think the real reason," said the cat, circling him and hissing, "is that you are a FOX!"

Sharpnose laughed and purred. "Well,

aren't you clever? Of course I am—but how ever did you guess? It will just be our little secret, won't it? Isn't it cream that you love? Cream and tuna?"

Zanzibar licked her lips and whiskers. "What do you know," she mewed, "about cream and tuna?"

"I know," purred the fox, "how to ask Aunt Zavella to give you all you want, you gorgeous creature."

"I'd like a fresh egg with that, *if* you don't mind," said Zanzibar. She rubbed against the fox's pant leg, and he scratched her behind the ears.

"You can have two eggs!" he sang, and they both ran up to the kitchen screen door and went inside.

Aunt Zavella was putting blue plates on the yellow kitchen table.

"Hi, Auntie," said the fox, exactly as he'd heard Martin say it.

Aunt Zavella smiled and looked at him. "Good evening, Martin," she said. "I was beginning to worry about you. You had a good walk?"

"Yes, Auntie, it was wonderful!" said the fox.

"Did you see anything interesting?" asked Martin's great aunt.

"I did! I saw the cleverest, most beautiful fox in the whole world!"

Aunt Zavella looked at him closely. "And were you careful, Martin," she asked, "when you looked at that fox?"

"I was extra-specially careful, Auntie!" said the fox with a smile. "You would have been proud of me. And now if you'll excuse me, I'll just run upstairs and—"

"But, Martin," said Aunt Zavella, "dinner's ready. Aren't you even a little hungry?"

"Hungry?" said the fox, who'd been so excited he'd forgotten how hungry he was. "I'm starving!"

"Well, good! I've made roast chicken and dumplings tonight."

"I'll have three chickens, please," said the fox, rushing to the table. Zanzibar rubbed against his legs. "Oh, yes, and two big bowls of tuna, cream, and eggs, please. One for our friend Zanzibar here, and one for me."

"Martin!" Aunt Zavella laughed. "You are such a tease! Usually you don't eat enough to keep a cricket alive!"

"I don't?"

"A bite of muffin for breakfast," said

Aunt Zavella. "A taste of peanut butter and jelly for lunch. And for supper . . . cinnamon honey cake!"

Of course, it was all the fox could do to keep from jumping onto the table and running off with the whole chicken. Being human with a fox's appetite is not easy, he thought. Aunt Zavella put a tiny piece of chicken on his plate and it was quickly gobbled up.

"You know," he said, licking his fork and fingers, "that *is* good! May I have just a little more, please?"

"You may have all you like!" beamed Aunt Zavella. Then she watched with surprise as the fox ate two chickens (one had been for the drive to the city the next day), twelve dumplings, a loaf of home-baked bread with half a pound of butter, all washed down with five glasses of milk. When he finished his fourth piece of blueberry pie, she cheered.

The fox belched, smiled happily, and licked his plate clean. He was startled at seeing his new face reflected in it.

"Your new appetite is wonderful, Martin," said his great aunt, "but what's become of your table manners?"

"Sorry, Auntie," said the fox, starting to get up. "Now if you'll excuse me, I'll run upstairs and—"

"I've got a great idea," Aunt Zavella said, rubbing her hands together. "How about a last game of badminton to work off all that food?"

"Badminton?" said the fox. He had watched Martin and his great aunt swat a little dead feathered thing back and forth

while they shouted at each other. Of all the stupid things they did, it seemed the stupidest.

"I think," he said, "I would prefer to just go upstairs and play my violin."

Aunt Zavella looked at him carefully. "You'd rather play your violin. . . than play badminton?"

"Well, actually. . ." The fox paused because he saw she was suspicious. "Actually. . ."

"Why not?" said Aunt Zavella. "Why shouldn't you play your fiddle if you want to?"

"Yes, why shouldn't I?" said the fox.

"No reason at all," said Aunt Zavella. "Play all you want, dear!"

"Thank you!" cried the fox, and he dashed up the stairs.

There, on the bed in Martin's room, was the battered violin case. From the first moment the fox had heard Martin play, the sound of the violin amazed him. It puzzled him. It tickled him. It made him absolutely happy.

Most foxes enjoy music, but this fox had a special passion for it. The only thing in the world more wonderful than hearing a violin, he thought, must be *playing* one!

Trembling with excitement, he opened the case and took out the violin. He raised it to his chin, just as he'd seen Martin do. Then he picked up the bow.

6

The Fox and the Fiddle

Downstairs, Aunt Zavella was talking on the telephone to Martin's parents in the city. They were getting ready to come pick up Martin the next morning.

"How is he?" asked Martin's mother.

"Is he all right?" asked his father on their second phone.

"He's fine," Aunt Zavella assured them. "He just ate two chickens, devoured almost a whole pie, and then ran upstairs to play his violin."

"Our Martin?" his parents cried together. "Eating two chickens? Playing the violin? What's happened to him?"

"There's no reason for worry," said Aunt Zavella. "It's perfectly normal. Here in the mountains people change. One day, they're one thing. The next day, they're something else. When I was a little girl in the Old Country—" She was interrupted by strange noises from upstairs.

"What's that screeching?" Martin's mother cried.

"Sounds like a cat caught in a vacuum cleaner!" said Martin's father.

"It sounds to me," said Aunt Zavella, "like a fox playing a fiddle. Have a good drive tomorrow. Martin and I are both looking forward to seeing you." And she quickly hung up the phone.

The fox ran down the stairs and into the kitchen. He held out the violin.

"There's something wrong with this

thing," he said. "It doesn't work!" He pulled the bow across the strings and produced the most hideous howls Aunt Zavella had ever heard.

"It needs fixing," said the frustrated fox.

"I can't see anything wrong with it," said Aunt Zavella. "Let me try. I used to play a little, years ago, in the Old Country." She took the fiddle and began to play a sweet, dreamy melody. It was the same tune Sharpnose had heard her sing so many times.

"Why doesn't it do that for me?" asked the fox.

Zanzibar, who had been chasing a mouse, stopped and listened to the music. The mouse stopped too, and then both it and Zanzibar began to waltz around the kitchen. Aunt Zavella started to sing:

Sleepy, sleepy baby
slipped into the gravy.
Baby's such a plump thing,
floated like a dumpling.
Grandma take your ladle,
and spoon him in his cradle.
Sweet, sleepy, sleepy eyes,
Auntie's baking baby pies,
to give the sleepy baby when
he opens up his eyes again. . . .

The old woman finished her song and the only sounds were the crickets creaking and the soft snoring of Zanzibar and the mouse, curled up together under the kitchen table.

"That was *beautiful*," sighed the fox.

"But why did they fall asleep?"

"It's an Old Country lullaby. It puts everyone to sleep," said Aunt Zavella, "*except* foxes. And you, Sharpnose, are a fox!"

"But, but..." sputtered the fox, "how do you know my name?"

"I've heard your mother calling you," chuckled Aunt Zavella. "In the Old Country, we learn the fox language in second grade."

"Well, aren't you clever," Sharpnose sneered. "But you *must* teach me to make that music!"

"I can't."

"Why not?"

"In the Old Country, we have an old saying—'Just because a fox steals a fiddle, it doesn't mean he can play a fandango.'"

"What does *that* mean?" snapped Sharpnose.

"It means foxes don't play fiddles."

"You MUST teach me!" he shrieked. "Ever since I heard Martin play, all I care about is music! I plotted and schemed just to have fingers to play that FIDDLE!"

"All right," said Aunt Zavella. "I'll try." But hard as she tried, it was no use. The fox's fiddling was awful.

"You are *not* a good teacher," he said.

"The only person who *might* be able to teach you," said Aunt Zavella, "is Martin. Where is he?"

"In the woods," cried Sharpnose, leaping to the door. "Let's find him! Hurry!"

"Zanzibar," said Aunt Zavella, "wake up and lead the way!"

The mouse continued snoring, but the

cat yawned, stretched, and sprang out the door. Aunt Zavella, playing a lively tune, followed into the last of the mountain twilight with Sharpnose right behind her.

The sky was pale lavender above the ridges. Overhead the first star appeared. Aunt Zavella fiddled on her way through the chicken yard. All the chickens danced in little circles till they were dizzy and toppled over.

Like toast from a toaster, a big fat moon popped up from the mountains, and Zanzibar dashed into the woods with Aunt Zavella and the fox dancing after her. Bats flitted about to the old woman's music and crickets sang along. Even fireflies flashed in time to its rhythm.

7

The Vixen

Meanwhile, deep in the woods in the body of a fox, Martin was having nothing but fun. He had chased dozens of chipmunks, squirrels, mice, and snakes. He didn't even care that he hadn't caught any. He had invaded the homes of woodchucks and rabbits, upset the nests of blackbirds, and laughed at their threats and curses.

Running through the evening as it deepened into night, he turned his ears in different directions, like dialing a radio. He heard owls and frogs, crickets and cicadas. Greetings, warnings, births, deaths, and weather reports bounced back and forth. The air hummed with the wild music of all these messages. Stars and fire-flies gave all the light he needed.

On a high rocky meadow under the roots of an old oak, Martin found a den full of three sweet-smelling baby foxes, all crying and calling for their mother. They were fat and woolly like tiny lambs.

Martin went in and made them laugh. He led them out onto the grass. They bounced and stumbled, and jumped all over him. He tumbled and rolled them over and over. They squealed and yapped with delight. The huge, dazzling moon rose into a raggedy sky, and Martin found a green snake under a rock for them to chase and bite and bat at.

"Martin?" said a voice so close that he jumped into the air and spun around.

A mother fox stood in the moonlight. The cubs let the snake slither off and ran to her calling, "Mammy! Mammy!"

A rabbit, its throat torn, lay on the ground in front of her. The smell of its thick, sweet blood made Martin dizzy. He suddenly realized he'd eaten nothing since a blueberry muffin at breakfast.

"How did you know my name?" asked the boy.

"My oldest son, Sharpnose, told me all about you and your fiddle," said the vixen. She lay down and let the cubs snuggle against her to nurse. "Oh, I warned him just like my mother warned me, 'Never look too long into the eyes of a human!' But, of course, he didn't listen."

"I'm glad," said Martin. "I love being a fox."

"Who wouldn't?" said the vixen. "That son of mine will get sick of being human soon enough. He's a fox, like I'm a fox, and foxes we'll remain."

"Me, too," said Martin. "I had to be human for nine whole years. There were some good parts, but being a fox is much better...." And he went on to tell her about all the things he'd done that day.

"Stop!" snapped the vixen. "Humans talk too much. Come on, babies," she said to her cubs, "into the den and we'll divide up this rabbit." She looked at Martin. "I can leave you a leg—or would you rather have the head?" she asked him.

"What for?" asked Martin.

"To eat, of course!"

"Oh, no," said Martin, "I only eat human food. Mostly cinnamon honey

cake, or peanut butter and jelly. You don't have any of those things, do you? I'm starving."

"Catch yourself a nice fat chipmunk," said the vixen, stuffing the rabbit into her den. "That's *real* food! Good luck!" The cubs scrambled in after it, and she followed them.

Martin started to join them but then wasn't sure he'd been invited. Can I be a real fox, he wondered, if I don't want to eat a chipmunk? Suddenly, he felt very alone and very hungry.

A breeze tickled the fur in his ears and whispered sounds from the woods below. He turned and sniffed the air—cinnamon honey cake and fiddle music were heading in his direction. Zanzibar galloped up the hill and stopped in front of him.

"Zanzibar!" said Martin. "Look! I'm a fox!"

"Are you sure?" purred Zanzibar. She sat and began to clean her paws. "I have a message from Aunt Zavella."

"What is it?"

"She says it's time to come home now."

8

The Music Lesson

"I'm not coming home," said Martin. "I love being a fox."

"I couldn't care less," said Zanzibar. "I'm just telling you what Aunt Zavella says."

"Yoo-hoo!" Aunt Zavella's voice was coming up the hill. "Yoo-hoo, Martin!"

"Aunt Zavella!" barked Martin, dashing up to her. "Wait till you hear all the things I've done. . . ."

"Look at you!" shrieked Sharpnose. "Look at the muddy mess you've made of *my* coat!. . . and *my* tail! All full of twigs and leaves and trash! You're ruining it!"

"I'll clean it later," said Martin, glancing at his coat and tail. They *were* a mess.

"You have to teach me to play your fiddle," said Sharpnose.

"How can I?" answered Martin. "I'm a fox now."

"Tell me how it's done."

"Practice," said Martin. "Practice, practice, practice."

"I *have* practiced. Teach me!" cried the fox.

"All right," said Martin. "I'll try."

Martin tried and tried. But Sharpnose's screeches only got worse. The night was slipping away. Sharpnose fell to the ground, beating his head on the dirt and weeping with frustration.

"Why can't *I* do it?" he wailed. "Why is everything human so *difficult?* Why is

water pouring from my eyes?" He held out the fiddle and bow to Martin. "You must *show* me how it's done!" Sharpnose demanded.

"You have my fingers," said Martin.

"Then we must change back. Just for a minute. Just till you show me the trick of it."

"Look how he's crying, Martin," said Aunt Zavella. She wiped Sharpnose's cheeks with her handkerchief and helped him blow his nose. "Don't you want to help him?"

"Do you promise," said Martin to Sharpnose, "that we will change right back again?"

"I promise."

"Cross your heart?"

"Cross my heart!"

So the fox boy crouched in front of Martin, and they looked into each other's eyes while Aunt Zavella sat on a mossy stone and whistled an Old Country tune.

In a few minutes, Martin was looking at a fox and not a boy, and he knew he was in his own body again. He stood up and stretched, wiggled his fingers, and scratched his head. It was like putting on comfortable old clothes after being in a Halloween costume, or getting into your own bed after sleeping in a strange one.

Sharpnose quickly began cleaning and grooming his coat and tail. "Just so it's not *quite* so disgusting," he said. Then he turned back to Martin, who had picked up the fiddle and bow. They felt so familiar in Martin's hands.

"It's done like this," Martin said. He

began to play and was surprised to find it was music he had never played before. "I seem to know this music," he said, "even though I never heard it before."

"Yes, it's beautiful," said Aunt Zavella. "It's about being a fox."

"Yes," said Martin. He shut his eyes while Sharpnose sat perfectly still and listened. The cubs and vixen looked out of their den and listened, too. Martin played and he heard the music sing to him:

The flame-red fox lives in the woods,
deep in his den lives he.
In a cleft in the rocks,
in a cave of earth,
under a hollow tree.
The flame-red fox runs in the woods,
on quick black feet runs he.

His eyes are yellow, his eyes are gold,
quick and gay and free.
Like a flash of fire, without a sound,
he stops to look at me.
If I could live another life,
a flame-red fox I'd be.
If I could live another life,
a flame-red fox I'd be.

The music ended on a long, soft, drawn-out howling note. All the foxes and Aunt Zavella howled along, softer and softer, until there was silence.

"Thank you, Martin," said Sharpnose. "You've taught me what I needed to know. People play violins, but I am a fox. A flame-red FOX! And a fox I will always be. Good-bye!" he barked and dashed into the woods.

But Martin could no longer understand him. He looked at Aunt Zavella and zipped up his jacket.

"It's getting cold," he said, "and I'm starving. Let's go home and have some cinnamon honey cake."

"And hot chocolate," said Aunt Zavella.

9

The Old Country

They started back through the woods. Zanzibar marched ahead, her tail held high. The moon was setting and the sky behind the mountains was blushing pink.

"I've never played the violin like that before," said Martin.

"You were never a fox before," said Aunt Zavella.

"Will I ever be a fox again?"

"Once a fox, always a fox, no matter what else you might be."

"Were you ever a fox, Auntie?"

"Of course. Years ago in the Old Country."

Whenever Aunt Zavella mentioned the Old Country, Martin pictured a land of cobwebs, worn carpets, and broken furniture.

"What *is* the Old Country?" he asked.

"The Old Country," said Aunt Zavella, "is where we aunts and uncles and grandmothers and grandfathers are always barefoot children. We play with lambs and baby goats in meadows full of crimson poppies. We wander in the woods—"

"Like these woods?"

"Exactly! And sometimes we glimpse tiny people in pointed caps. And sometimes we meet deer that speak to us, or foxes that want to play our fiddles. The Old Country is where nothing is only one thing and everything can be anything. The Old Country is where all the stories come from."

The first morning bird began to sing. A cardinal. Then a second and a third—a robin and a chickadee. Martin and Aunt Zavella and Zanzibar walked over the dewy grass to the house.

They drank hot chocolate and ate cinnamon honey cake while Martin told of his adventures.

And late that afternoon, while Aunt Zavella waved good-bye from the porch and a fox watched from where the woods shadowed the grass, Martin and his parents began their drive back to the city.

10
Magic

Sharpnose saw Martin get into the big metal thing. He heard its doors slam shut and then heard the people call to each other as the thing moved mysteriously away.

The old woman stood on the porch, waving her scarf long after the sounds of the thing were gone. Zanzibar perched on the railing, licking her fur. Except for a few sleepy chickadees, the mountains were quiet.

Sharpnose was glad not to be human. He remembered the pain of not being able to play the fiddle and shuddered. But he was surprised at how much he missed the music. Life seemed empty without it.

"Hello, Sharpnose!" said a voice. "I bet you miss the music, eh?"

It was the old woman. She had a perfect fox accent. Sharpnose looked at her and laughed.

"I always suspected you were part fox!" he said. "Yes, I miss the music."

"I miss it, too," said Aunt Zavella. "And I miss Martin. But look what he left me." She picked up the old violin case from the porch. "His parents got him a new one, and they gave this one back to me."

She took out the fiddle and plucked at the strings, tuning them. The fox found himself moving closer, inch by inch, until Zanzibar puffed herself up and hissed, *"Close enough!"*

The fox sat at the foot of the stairs. He felt a tingle of excitement.

"What would you like to hear?" the old woman asked him.

Sharpnose jumped up. "Would you play the one about being a fox? The one that Martin played?"

"Ah, yes," she chuckled. "I know that one well from the Old Country."

Aunt Zavella raised her bow and began to play. A wave of warmth spread through Sharpnose's body. It was happiness and sadness all mixed together.

The music of the violin floated up and out over the mountains. The sun faded away and the moon rose slowly, like a huge, silver balloon.

The old woman played and the fox listened.

"Oh, Aunt Zavella," he sighed, "how do you humans do it? How do you make music?"

"It's magic," she said. And played on.

About the Author

Mordicai Gerstein's favorite animal is the fox. He sometimes spots foxes near his home in Massachusetts. "They are not afraid. A fox will look you right in the eye," Mordicai says. "It's a magical moment."

Mordicai is a painter, sculptor, and filmmaker, but he's best known for the books he's written and illustrated for kids. They include *Stop Those Pants!* and *The Wild Boy*, a *New York Times* Best Illustrated Book of the Year.

Do you like books about animals?
You may also want to read

Ghost Horse
by George Edward Stanley

Emily got out of bed. She ran to the
window and pulled back the curtains. In
the moonlight, she could see the beautiful white horse!

Emily pinched herself. "Ouch!" Now
she knew she wasn't dreaming. The
beautiful white horse was really there!

He started walking toward her window.
But the closer he got, the paler he got.

Emily gasped. She could see through
the horse!

"You're . . . you're a ghost!" she whispered.